Rosie and Jim™

The
Big Fish

Written by Robin Stevens

Illustrations by Helen Prole

Designed by Mark Boardman

Ragdoll
works for children

MADCAP

On a sleepy old canal there was a boat.
On that boat was a wooden duck.
"Quack!" said the duck. "Quack quack!"

Two old ragdolls woke up inside the boat.

One was called Rosie and the other Jim.
"Let's go!" said Rosie.
"Yes, come on!" said Jim.

And off they went. "Quack,
wait for me!" said Duck.

One day, Rosie and Jim went for a walk beside a small stream.

Suddenly, they heard a loud SPLASH and there, swimming
in the water beside them, was a very large fish.
"Look at that big fish, Rosie!" said Jim.

"Hello, big fish," said Rosie.
"Blub-blub, blub-blub," said the fish.
"Pardon me?" asked Jim.
"I think he said, 'Blub-blub, blub-blub,'" answered Rosie.
"Oh I see," said Jim. "What does that mean?"

"Quack-quack-quack, quack-quack-quack,
quackety-quack!" said Duck.
"Oh," said Rosie. "Duck said that the big fish wants to
know if we'd like a ride all the way down the small
stream to the end of the long, long river!"

"Oooh, lovely!" said Jim. "A ride all the way down the small stream to the end of the long, long river."
"Yes, please," said Rosie.
So Rosie and Jim climbed on to the comfortable back of the big fish and floated off down the stream.
"Quack, wait for me!" said Duck.

Before long, a small fish came up to Rosie and Jim.
"Where are you going?" asked the small fish.
"We're going all the way down the small stream to the end of the long, long river," replied Rosie and Jim.

"To the end of the long, long river?" said the small fish.
"May I swim along as well? I'm so tired of this small stream."

"Yes, why not?" said Rosie and Jim.
The small fish joined on behind and they all
swam together down the small stream.
"Quack, wait for me!" said Duck.

Next, they met a small frog.
"Where are you all going?" asked the small frog.
"We're swimming all the way down the small stream to the end of the long, long river," replied Rosie and Jim.
"To the end of the long, long river?" said the small frog.
"May I swim along as well? I'm so tired of this small stream."

"Yes, why not?" said Rosie and Jim.
The small frog joined on behind and they all
swam together down the small stream.
"Quack, wait for me!" called Duck.

A young swan saw them all coming and could not believe her eyes.
"Where are you all going?" she asked.
"We're swimming all the way down the small stream to the end of the long, long river," replied Rosie and Jim.
"To the end of the long, long river?" said the young swan.
"May I swim along as well? I'm so tired of this small stream."

"Yes, why not?" said Rosie and Jim.
So the young swan joined on behind and they all swam on together down the small stream. "Quack, wait for me!" called Duck.

Soon, the small stream became a much bigger stream.
"Oooh, this is better than our small stream," said the small fish.

"I want to see the long, long river!" cried Rosie.
"Come on, let's go then!" laughed Jim.
"Quack!" said Duck.
So the big fish swam on down the stream until...

...at last they all reached the long, long river.

"Hooray, we did it!" said Jim.

"But I want to see the end of the long, long river," said Rosie.

"Oh Rosie, you noggin!" said Jim.

"Quack!" said Duck.

So the big fish swam on down the long, long river.
They swam past Rosie and Jim's boat.
"Quack!" said Duck.

The big fish swam past trees.
"Big trees!" said the small fish.
The big fish swam past houses.
"Big houses!" said the small frog.
They all swam past a mountain.
"Big mountain!" said the young swan.

Finally, they reached the end of the long, long river.
"Hooray!" said Rosie.
"We did it. We've come all the way to the sea!" said Jim.

"Ooh, the sea is very big!" said the small fish.
"Ooh, the sea is very big!" said the small frog.
"Ooh, the sea is very big!" said the young swan.

"I think we ought to go back now, Rosie," said Jim.
"The sea *is* very big!" agreed Rosie.

So they all swam back up the long, long river as fast as they could...

...all the way back to the small stream.
"I like our nice, small stream," said the small fish.
"Yes, we like our nice small stream as well," said the small frog and the young swan.

"Thanks for the lovely ride, big fish," said Rosie and Jim.
The big fish gave them a big, wet kiss and then
disappeared back under the water again with a SPLASH!

Rosie and Jim set off back to their boat.
"Quack, wait for me!" called Duck.

Rosie and Jim gave each other a big kiss and
then all was quiet on the boat again.

The wooden duck did not make a sound.
All that could be heard was the soft
rippling of the water against the side of
the canal boat.

Other Rosie and Jim titles available from Madcap:
Music Party
The Biggest Mess Ever (A Sticker Storybook)

The Big Fish and **Music Party** are also available as book and tape
from MCI Children's Audio

A Video of **Music Party** is available from VCI

Text and illustrations copyright © 1998 Madcap Books
First published in Great Britain in 1998 by Madcap Books, André Deutsch Ltd,
76 Dean Street, London, W1V 5HA
André Deutsch is a subsidiary of VCI plc
www.vci.co.uk

Rosie and Jim copyright © 1998 Ragdoll Productions (UK) Ltd.
Design of the Rosie and Jim puppets and photographic dolls copyright
© Ragdoll Productions (UK) Ltd.
Based on a Ragdoll Production for ITV. All rights reserved.

A catalogue record for this title is available from the British Library.
ISBN 0 233 99272 3

All rights reserved. This book is sold subject to the condition that it may not be
reproduced, stored in a retrieval system, or transmitted in any form or by any means,
electronic, mechanical, photocopying, recording or otherwise, without the publisher's
prior consent.

Printed in the UK